THROUGH THESE LINES

Sisters' lines, No. 3 Australian General Hospital, Lemnos.
The morning after a storm.

Photo: A.W. Savage. Mitchell Library, State Library of New South Wales, PXE 698.

Through These Lines

A PLAY IN 5 ACTS BY
CHERYL WARD

LITTLE GULLY PUBLISHING

2024

Play script

© copyright Cheryl Ward

Cover design by Cheryl Ward. Includes her photo of stained-glass
window 'Devotion' by Napier Wallace in the Hall of Memory
of the Australian War Memorial, and ephemera from her collection.
Red cross image by Di Mackey.

Second edition, April 2024

ISBN 978-0-6459276-5-8 (paperback)
ISBN 978-0-6459276-6-5 (ebook)

Little Gully Publishing
littlegully.com

A catalogue record for this
book is available from the
National Library of Australia

Production rights

For the right to perform this play, and copy licenses, contact Cheryl Ward
office@norestforthewicked.net

CONTENTS

No. 2 Australian General Hospital, Mena House, Cairo.
The first batch of Australian wounded from the Gallipoli landings.

PRODUCTION HISTORY

2010, Headland Park, Mosman, Sydney

First performed in the underground ammunition store of the
19th century military fortifications at Georges Heights, Mosman.

Produced by No Rest For The Wicked (Cheryl Ward).
Directed by Cheryl Ward. Set Tom Bannerman, sound Jeremy Silver,
costumes Cassie Pascoli, lights Sprios Hristias.

With Coralie Bywater as Flo, Mairead Berne as Sister Douglas *et al*,
Lucy Miller as Matron Watson *et al*, Johann Walraven as Lt Davies
et al, Peter Whitehead as Colonel McLean *et al* and Sebastian Lamour
as Private Jenkins *et al*.

2014, New South Wales regional tour

Produced by TTL Productions (Cheryl Ward and Paul Whiteley).
Directed by Mary-Anne Gifford. Set Tom Bannerman, sound Alistair
Wallace, lights Elliot Glass, costumes Alison Whiteford.

With Kate Skinner as Flo, Rebecca Barbera as Sister Douglas *et al*,
Cheryl Ward as Matron Watson *et al*, Gareth Rickards at Lt Davies *et
al*, Gary Clementson as Colonel McLean *et al* and Christian Charisiou
as Private Jenkins *et al*.

2015, Casula Powerhouse Arts Centre residency, Anzac Day (Liverpool City Council), Greek Festival of Sydney

Produced by TTL Productions (Cheryl Ward and Paul Whiteley).
Directed by Cheryl Ward. Set Tom Bannerman, sound Alistair Wallace,
lights Elliot Glass, costumes Alison Whiteford.

With Emily Kennedy as Flo, Chloe Schwank as Sister Douglas *et al*,
Cheryl Ward as Matron Watson *et al*, Ben Simpson as Lt Davies *et al*,
Donald Sword as Colonel McLean *et al* and Alex Thompson as
Private Jenkins *et al*.

Abridged version, titled 'Through These Lines: Towards Lemnos',
presented in association with Lemnos1915 and the Lemnian
Association of NSW at the 2015 Greek Festival of Sydney.

CHARACTERS IN ORDER OF FIRST APPEARANCE

All characters are Australian unless otherwise indicated.

Aboard *Kyarra*

Sister Mary Douglas (30 years of age)

Private Harold Jenkins (18)

Private Stanley Skinner (35)

Sister Florence Whiting — 'Flo' (27)

Matron Ada Watson (40)

Captain Charles McLean (45)

Cairo

Staff Nurse April Guilford (23)

Lieutenant William Davies (35)

Private William Corkhill (19)

VD patient

Aboard *Gascon*

Major James Forrest (English — Received Pronunciation)

Sister Hilda Smith (English — Yorkshire)

Orderly Barrie (English — London)

Matron Simcox (English — Received Pronunciation)

Yilmaz Onbaşı (Turkish)

Capitaine Joseph Cagnet (French)

Patient A (imagined — pulped arm and upper torso wounds)

Patient B (shattered humerus)

Patient C (forearm gutter wound)

Patient D (shattered jaw, walking wounded)

Patient E (broken ankle)

Patient F (imagined — haemorrhaging abdomen)

Orderly #1

Patient G (imagined — chest wound)

Orderly #2

Patient H (imagined — head wound)

Patient I (imagined — penetrating shoulder)

Patient J (imagined — neck, entry and exit wound)

Chaplain (voice only)

Lemnos

Piper

Colonel Arthur Frances

Patient #2 (New Zealander)

Patient #1 (English — Cockney)

Captain Archibald Barnes

Batman to Colonel Frances

Patient (naval stoker, stage manager or imagined)

France: Wimereux and Blendecques

Sister Eunice Laffin (Canadian)

Wimereux orderly

Mr Neville Whiting

Canadian officer

Anzac soldiers (voices only)

Major Wallace Leonard (Canadian)

Matron Katherine Hall (Canadian)

Colonel Edward Terrey

Sergeant Little — 'Shorty' (Irish)

American soldier

Going on duty, No. 3 Australian General Hospital.
Abbassia, Cairo, 1916.

SUGGESTED CHARACTER DOUBLING

Cast of 6 (3F/3M)

The 2014 and 2015 productions used the following character doubling.

Actor 1

Sister Florence Whiting — 'Flo'.

Actor 2

Sister Mary Douglas, Staff Nurse April Guilford, Matron Simcox, Matron Katherine Hall.

Actor 3

Matron Ada Watson, Sister Hilda Smith, Sister Eunice Laffin.

Actor 4

Private Stanley Skinner, Captain Charles McLean, VD patient, Major James Forrest, *Capitaine* Cagnet, Patient #1, Colonel Frances, Mr Neville Whiting, Major Wallace Leonard, Colonel Edward Terrey, extra soldier (influenza patient) in final scene of Act 5.

Actor 5

Private Harold Jenkins, Private William Corkhill, Orderly Barrie, Yilmaz Onbaşı, Patients B & D, Orderly #2, Lieutenant Archibald Barnes, Patient #2, Batman to Colonel Frances, Wimereux orderly, Canadian officer, Sergeant Little, American soldier.

Actor 6

Lieutenant William Davies, Patients C & E, Orderly #1.

Stage manager or imagined

Patient (naval stoker).

Troops on board HMAT *Euripides* prior to departure, 8 May 1915.
A group of nurses stand at the rail.

Photo: Josiah Barnes. Australian War Memorial, PB0381.

Bandaging class, RMS *Mooltan*, 1915.

Photo: A.W. Savage. Mitchell Library, State Library of NSW, PXE 698.

ACT ONE | SCENE 1

Aboard the hospital ship Kyarra, *docked at the Union Wharf, SYDNEY.*

Bright sunny afternoon. 4pm, 28 November 1914.

Ship's horn sounds three times as a farewell. Soldiers and nurses jostle on board the packed deck to get to the ship's rails.

SISTER MARY DOUGLAS, PRIVATE JENKINS and PRIVATE SKINNER are waving and throwing streamers towards their loved ones down on the wharf. All but SISTER FLORENCE WHITING (FLO) are laden with packages and farewell gifts. PRIVATE JENKINS also carries bags of cherries and oranges.

Ship's engines are at full steam as it moves away from the wharf. Cheering, band music and seagulls add to the cacophony. Streamers snap.

JENKINS	Shimmy over, love, let a man in. Here Gran, here! OVER HERE!
SISTER DOUGLAS	Can you see a woman in a green hat?
FLO	There?
SISTER DOUGLAS	Yes! *(Calling to her family)* Stay where I can see you, Mum. *(Holding up a package)* What's in it? I won't open it before Christmas. *(To FLO)* You're in my cabin. My name is Mary.
FLO	Florence.
SISTER DOUGLAS	The cabin isn't very appealing, is it? We're packed in like sardines. And all these men. Never seen so many.
FLO	Yes, it's quite overwhelming.
SKINNER	*(From the rigging)* What? I will, I will! I can look after myself, don't you worry!

MATRON WATSON enters.

MATRON WATSON	*(To Skinner)* Get down Private. You'll hurt yourself.
SKINNER	Keep your hat on Sister.
MATRON WATSON	Matron — Miss Watson — get down, you'll break your neck.
JENKINS	GRAN! OVER HERE! Yes, hello!
SKINNER	No worries, I was a circus performer in my youth.

SKINNER swings effortlessly down and disappears into the crowd.

MATRON WATSON	Where's your commanding officer?

MATRON WATSON exits.

JENKINS	I will — I WILL BRING BACK A MUMMY. A MUMMY!
	(To SISTER DOUGLAS whose streamers have entangled him) Deaf as a post. Not you, my grandmother. We seem to have got all tangled up.
	Name is Harry, Harold Jenkins, but you can call me Hal, Jenko, Jenks, sweetheart — anything that takes ya fancy, and what would be your lovely name?
SISTER DOUGLAS	Mary Douglas, but you can call me Sister Douglas.

SISTER DOUGLAS takes FLO by the arm and moves away.

	(To FLO) It was Flo, wasn't it? Where are you from? I was born in Goulburn but we moved to Sydney when I was fifteen.

SKINNER (*To JENKINS*) No luck with that one then? Stanley Skinner.

JENKINS Harry Jenkins.

SISTER DOUGLAS (*To FLO*) Trained at the Royal Prince Alfred. You?

FLO Lithgow Base — the ship's quite unsteady already, isn't it?

SISTER DOUGLAS No, it's fine.

JENKINS Any suggestions?

SKINNER These older women are tough. Gotta go softly, softly.

SISTER DOUGLAS (*Waving to her family in the crowd*) Anyone seeing you off?

FLO My family couldn't — the ship is rocking. (*FLO rushes to the railings to retch*)

JENKINS After you. (*Skinner ponders his line of approach*)

SISTER DOUGLAS I'm glad I took the top berth. Take a deep breath — wave to your — to someone…

SKINNER (*To FLO and SISTER DOUGLAS*) Private Stanley Skinner.

JENKINS Private Harold Jenkins. (*To SISTER DOUGLAS*) Hello again. Cherry? (*SISTER DOUGLAS ignores him*) Orange?

MATRON WATSON re-enters and watches her new Sisters.

SKINNER (*To FLO*) Noticed you looked a little out of sorts and just thought I could help you —

FLO No, thank you.

SISTER DOUGLAS	She's fine.
SKINNER	She doesn't look well at all to me — I'm not a doctor but —
MATRON WATSON	Are you fit for this journey, Sister?
FLO	Yes, Miss Watson.
SKINNER	Just a bit of sea sickness, Matron.
MATRON WATSON	Thank you, Private. We haven't even left the harbour yet, Sister Whiting.
FLO	I'll be all right — once we're on our way —
MATRON WATSON	You'll need to be. This isn't a pleasure cruise.
SKINNER	No worries, it's a long voyage. We've all the time in the world to get acquainted.
JENKINS	Yes, we have weeks — months, I hear.
SKINNER	Right well then, Sis — Mayyy — Missssswatson must be off... Have to see a man about a dog.

SKINNER and JENKINS back away.

JENKINS	I think Matron likes you...

SKINNER and JENKINS climb the rigging. Ship's horn blasts three times. They all take their last look.

	Bye Gran, you lovely deaf old thing, I'm gunna miss you.
SKINNER	Think my family was happy to see me go.
SISTER DOUGLAS	They're too far away now, I can't see them.
MATRON WATSON	Never mind. It's a wonderful afternoon to be heading off.

ACT ONE | SCENE 2

Aboard the hospital ship Kyarra, *off the south coast of* AUSTRALIA.

Ship's dispensary, mid-morning, early December 1914.

MATRON WATSON holds the first aid manual. FLO and SISTER DOUGLAS hold a helmet and bandages. The men practice callisthenic drills on the shelter deck.

MATRON WATSON	(*Reading from manual*) Capeline bandage for the head. You'll need the double-headed roller bandage. Apply the bandage to the forehead with the lower edge just above the eyebrows. A little lower, Sister Whiting.
FLO	Yes, Miss Watson.
MATRON WATSON	Carry each end to the back of the head, over the temples, crossing the ends — good, Sister Douglas. You've done this before.
SISTER DOUGLAS	No, Miss.
MATRON WATSON	The upper bandage is continued onwards around the head whilst the lower is brought upwards over the centre of the top of the scalp as far as the root of the nose. The bandage that encircles —

FLO drops her bandage end.

	Start again, catch up. Do I need to go a little slower, Sister Whiting?
FLO	No, I'm —
MATRON WATSON	Seasick? Distracted by the men perhaps?
FLO	Not at all, Miss Watson.

MATRON WATSON   Very soon their lives may depend on the skills you're learning here today.

FLO   *(Close to tears)* I know that —

MATRON WATSON   The bandage that encircles the head is then brought over the forehead, covering the bandages that traverse the scalp. Thus fixing the latter in place.

The turns are continued, the scalp end of the bandage passing alternatively backwards and forwards, first one side, then at the other of the central fold, until the whole scalp is covered.

To finish, both ends are carried 'round the head horizontally above the ears and pinned off.

Good. Again.

ACT ONE | SCENE 3

Aboard the hospital ship Kyarra *off the east coast of AFRICA.*

Ship's dispensary, late afternoon, 20 December 1914.

FLO is folding bandages. Sister Douglas pokes her head around the corner.

SISTER DOUGLAS	Anything exciting happening? They have me doing inventory in Supplies, alone. I still need to practise the double shoulder, don't seem to be able to do it as tightly as you.
FLO	You know you're much better at all the bandages than I am —
SISTER DOUGLAS	You seem impervious to the men's attentions.
FLO	I'm not impervious. I'm here to do a job.
SISTER DOUGLAS	Do you have anyone special at home?
FLO	Miss Watson is on her rounds, Mary.
SISTER DOUGLAS	I'm bored.
FLO	If she finds you here again —
SISTER DOUGLAS	She'll blame you for being a bad influence!
	I'd already read all my mail before we'd even left Durban... Why haven't you written home? I've sent seven — no eight.
FLO	They'll be busy with the preparations for Daisy's — for my sister's wedding.
SISTER DOUGLAS	You're missing your sister's wedding? Don't you want to know how it went? Write home, then you can tell me all about it —
JENKINS	*(Singing softly from corridor)* Oh you beautiful doll, you great big beautiful doll...

JENKINS enters wearing cherries on his ears, followed by SKINNER who stands guard at the door.

	Who have we got here? Well now, what luck…
SKINNER	Afternoon, ladies.
SISTER DOUGLAS	I have to get back to Supplies. But Flo is staying…
FLO	Miss Watson is on her rounds.
SKINNER	Oh, she loves me.
JENKINS	Got her wrapped around his little finger, he has. Speaking of fingers. Mary, I'm injured.
SISTER DOUGLAS	I'm not on duty, Harold, you'll have to show Flo.
JENKINS	Fine, I'll show Flo. *(To FLO)* I'm suffering.
FLO	There is no obvious injury.
JENKINS	It's muscular.
FLO	Does this hurt?
JENKINS	Agony.
FLO	This?
JENKINS	Excruciating. Wait a minute, it's spreading — there's so many of them.
SISTER DOUGLAS	Perhaps you should bandage it, Flo. Or cut it off.
FLO	Harry, it's fine. You should go.

FLO moves him along.

JENKINS	Thought you nurses were supposed to care… *(To SKINNER)* Next!

SKINNER moves in close to FLO.

SKINNER   Sister Whiting, I've got a stiff... neck.

SISTER DOUGLAS   The masseuse is down the corridor.

SKINNER   Wisdom from the wings.

FLO   The masseuse is down the corridor.

FLO moves him out.

SKINNER   You're lovely, you know. Even with a
                           handkerchief on ya head.

JENKINS   *(To FLO)* Especially with a handkerchief on
                           ya head. Sets off your eyes. So blue. And so
                           would these.

JENKINS pushes in and puts a simple beaded necklace,
a souvenir of Colombo, around FLO's neck. SKINNER and SISTER
DOUGLAS are not impressed.

SKINNER   I thought that was for —

JENKINS   Flo mate, Flo.

FLO   *(Confused)* For me? Thank you.

SISTER DOUGLAS   What is it?

SISTER DOUGLAS moves in for a closer look.

FLO   A necklace.

SKINNER   Don't you worry, Mary, I've had one for you
                           all along...

SKINNER puts the beaded necklace around SISTER DOUGLAS' neck.

SISTER DOUGLAS   Well, thank you Stanley.

SISTER DOUGLAS kisses SKINNER on his cheek.

JENKINS   Steady on, mate.

                           Right then...

JENKINS kisses FLO on the cheek.

FLO   You...

FLO hits JENKINS with a nearby medical item and chases him away.

JENKINS   Well, that's a fine response from my Flo.

SISTER DOUGLAS   Your Flo? I thought I was your Mary?

SISTER DOUGLAS begins to chase and hit JENKINS with a nearby medical item.

JENKINS   You are, you are, I'm just spreading the love. I have a lot to give. If you are not careful I am going to have to discipline you unruly Sisters.

SKINNER   Agreed, I think sanctions are called for.

FLO   Oh, no, please, not sanctions.

SKINNER   You women are a disgrace to the profession...

JENKINS   A good hiding is in order!

JENKINS goes to smack SISTER DOUGLAS on the bottom.

SISTER DOUGLAS   *(Whacks his hand)* Get out of it.

JENKINS   Hey, watch it, that's me wounded hand — finger — nah, it's the whole hand now... How will I ever dance with my Mary again?

SISTER DOUGLAS   *(She stops)* Well you won't!

JENKINS   (*Crashing into her*) A low blow. First my finger
                                 is ignored and now my heart. How could you
                                 knock a man when he's down? You should
                                 be taking me in your arms. Be feeding me
                                 grapes.

JENKINS 'faints' into SISTER DOUGLAS' arms, she steps aside,
he lands heavily.

SISTER DOUGLAS   I didn't think you would actually throw
                                 yourself... (*She tries to help him up*) That fall
                                 was hard, you goose, are you all right?

SKINNER   He's fine! We should dance!

SKINNER scoops FLO up and twirls her around the room. JENKINS
tries to kiss SISTER DOUGLAS and she pushes him back down.

JENKINS   Steady on, no need to get violent. Numb
                                 finger, numb hand, numb heart — it is
                                 spreading! Through me whole body,
                                 something's wrong with me legs. Now me
                                 eyes are going — tell Gran I love her fruit
                                 cake. Mary, my Mary, where are you my girl?
                                 Who turned out the lights? Mary, is that you?

JENKINS reaches out to touch SISTER DOUGLAS' breasts.

SISTER DOUGLAS   Thought you said your hand was numb?

FLO   Harold Jenkins!

MATRON WATSON enters.

MATRON WATSON   Out of here now!

SKINNER runs to the exit.

JENKINS   *(Taking a cherry from his pocket, offering it to MATRON WATSON)* Cherry?

JENKINS exits.

                   (Singing) You great big beautiful doll...

MATRON WATSON   This is the ship's dispensary and not a brothel. You should be ashamed of yourselves.

FLO   It's just harmless fun, Miss Watson. We would never —

SISTER DOUGLAS   *(To FLO)* Speak for yourself!

MATRON WATSON   You're as bad as the men. *(To SISTER DOUGLAS)* Get back to Supplies.

MATRON WATSON exits.

ACT ONE | SCENE 4

Aboard the hospital ship Kyarra, *off the east coast of AFRICA.*

On deck, mid-morning, early January 1915.

The nurses enter, rushing into formation. They wear very large life vests. The soldiers can be heard cheering the arrival of the nursing sisters.

MATRON WATSON   Move up, Sisters, move in. Keep coming until we're all in… that's it.

CAPTAIN McLEAN enters.

Captain McLean! The sisters have done very well at the drills this morning.

CAPT McLEAN   Yes, finally — aft to promenade deck in some sort of time that may prevent disaster — and it only took a month. Remember — urgency, yes — panic, never. Preparation and discipline are the key.

MATRON WATSON   Yes, they are.

CAPT McLEAN   Disappointingly, I have been reminded how frail that discipline can be. After the leniency shown to you over Christmas and the new year, many of the nursing staff continue to fraternise with the men.

The soldiers cheer in approval.

This is unacceptable behaviour.

MATRON WATSON   Yes, discipline needs to be re-established.

CAPT McLEAN   Well, I'm glad you agree Matron, because from now on the nursing staff are confined to the promenade deck, wards and their cabins only.

The soldiers groan with disappointment.

	Any breach of these orders will result in disciplinary action and curfews...
MATRON WATSON	Are the men to be confined?
CAPT McLEAN	The men need to move freely about the ship, Matron — they're not your concern. They're away from their families, tensions are high —
MATRON WATSON	We're living together under such — well, in extremely close quarters. The men are still in such boisterous spirits.
CAPT McLEAN	The men have a vital task ahead and must not be distracted from it. To put it simply Miss Watson, your nurses need to obey orders. You are dismissed.

MATRON WATSON   We have received our orders, we'll be splitting
                     up, for the moment.

SISTER DOUGLAS   That's a shame.

FLO   Why?

MATRON WATSON   They're our orders.

                     Sister Douglas, you'll go to Heliopolis with
                     the First. Sister Whiting and I will be with the
                     Second, at Mena House, next to the pyramids.
                     Others are going to Choubra and Alexandria.
                     It's only temporary — until everything is
                     running smoothly, then I'm sure we'll all
                     be back together as a unit. We dock early.

MATRON WATSON exits. She spots JENKINS hiding in the corridor.

                     Get back to your cabin, now!

JENKINS   Yes, Sir, Matron!

JENKINS scurries below deck.

FLO   She's splitting us up. She's been in
                     McLean's ear.

SISTER DOUGLAS   Miss Watson? She'd have no say in it.

FLO   Aren't you upset they're splitting us up?

SISTER DOUGLAS   Of course, but we didn't come here
                     to make friends.

*SISTER DOUGLAS grabs a few items of toiletries and a lantern and
exits.*

FLO   No... I didn't come to make friends. Why
                     did I come? I'm not sorry. This is where
                     I should be. Will they ever understand that?

FLO picks up the pen, about to write, but puts it down...

Nurse and patient at Mena House, Cairo, 1915.
Photo: David Izatt. National Library of Australia, nla.obj-141329329.

ACT TWO | SCENE 1

2nd Australian General Hospital, Mena House, CAIRO, EGYPT.

8am, 25 January 1915.

STAFF NURSE GUILFORD races in… she looks around the dispensary.

SN GUILFORD	Is…?
FLO	Don't worry, Miss Watson isn't here yet.
SN GUILFORD	Oh good. I'm Sister Guilford. April.
FLO	Sister Whiting. Florence.

MISS WATSON enters.

MATRON WATSON	Sister Whiting, Sister Guilford, you found the dispensary, good. Mena House is —
SN GUILFORD	It's very beautiful.
MATRON WATSON	A bit of a labyrinth.
FLO	The pyramids are across the road.
MATRON WATSON	Ah, so you've had a chance to walk around then.
FLO	No Miss, you can see them from our window.
SN GUILFORD	Queen Mary banqueted here.
MATRON WATSON	That's very interesting, Sister Guilford.
FLO	So we get to dine in a palace too.
MATRON WATSON	It was a hotel and now it's a hospital.
FLO	Yes, Miss Watson.
MATRON WATSON	So, on this floor there are twenty small wards with four beds in each. Most are empty at the moment.

In the east wing wards, we have a few simple fractures — arms, wrists, ankles and a compound fracture of the femur. Climbing the pyramids. The west wing wards are for dysentery and we have three appendicitis and two tonsils, all recovering well from surgery.

Nurses' station is at the centre of the corridor, orderlies' station is by the eastern stairs. You will have a male orderly on duty with you at all times. The native helpers are by the outbuildings. They will fetch you water and linen and sweep but not much else. Their English is non-existent.

Kitchen and bathing facilities are in the basement. And there is no need for you to access the wards on the upper floor, the male orderlies are on duty there.

FLO   Why, Miss Watson?

MATRON WATSON   Because they are taken up with the clap. *(STAFF NURSE GUILFORD has no idea what the clap is)* Gonorrhea. *(STAFF NURSE GUILFORD knows that name)* As I said, the male orderlies are on duty there. But I thought this morning, before our rounds, we'd ensure the dispensary was fully stocked, so this —

An Australian, LIEUTENANT WILLIAM DAVIES, enters.

Good morning, Lieutenant, how can we help you?

LT DAVIES   Good morning, sisters. I've cut my hand — a small cut but —

MATRON WATSON   Come in, sit down. Sister Whiting,
                     can you see what we have by way of plasters
                     for small cuts…

FLO   Yes, Miss.

MATRON WATSON examines LT DAVIES' hand.

MATRON WATSON   And it will need to be cleaned. Sister
                     Guilford.

SN GUILFORD   Yes, Miss.

SISTER GUILFORD gets a basin and washes the wound with liquid.

MATRON WATSON   Actually Sister Whiting, the webbing
                     is split, you will need a bandage. No need for
                     sutures though.

LT DAVIES   Glad to hear it.

*SN GUILFORD and FLO attend to LT DAVIES who watches
FLO throughout.*

MATRON WATSON   How has your morning been, Lieutenant?

LT DAVIES   Despite my hand, it's shaping up to be a very
                     good morning.

MATRON WATSON   Glad to hear it. Yes, the mornings here are
                     lovely, but I'm not looking forward to the heat
                     of summer though.

LT DAVIES   Not sure we'll still be here, Sister.

MATRON WATSON   I'm matron, Miss Watson.

LT DAVIES   Forgive me, Miss Watson.

FLO continues to bandage —

MATRON WATSON	How are we going there? It's just a small cut.
FLO	Almost finished.
LT DAVIES	She's being very thorough.
MATRON WATSON	Yes.

FLO finishes the bandage.

LT DAVIES	(*Quietly to FLO*) Marry me?
	Or a walk to the pyramids at least? The Sphinx?
MATRON WATSON	Lieutenant, you're finished, you can go.
LT DAVIES	Davies, Matron…

LT DAVIES calls back as he exits.

Lieutenant William Davies.

ACT TWO | SCENE 2

Fracture ward, 2AGH, Mena House, CAIRO, EGYPT.

2am, 28 March 1915.

STAFF NURSE GUILFORD is attending PRIVATE CORKHILL who has a broken femur in a splint. The other patients sleep. She works by lantern light. She is tired and trying not to fall asleep. She fails for a moment.

PTE CORKHILL   It's lovely there, though. Should be a great day for everyone.

A sound wakes her.

SN GUILFORD   What?

PTE CORKHILL   Have you been asleep the whole time I was talking to you?

SN GUILFORD   Sorry Corkhill, I heard most of it. Sleep now, you can tell me the rest tomorrow night.

PTE CORKHILL   If I stop talking I feel the pain. Can you stop it from hurtin'? Loosen it? Please?

VD PATIENT   *(Calling — off)* Sssssssssssiiisssstaaaa?

SN GUILFORD   I can't loosen it. When was your last morphia injection?

STAFF NURSE GUILFORD checks his chart to confirm.

PTE CORKHILL   Before dinner.

SN GUILFORD   Alright. I'll be a minute.

She goes out to the nurses' station.

VD PATIENT	*(Off)* Sisssta.
SN GUILFORD	*(Quietly — off)* You should be asleep, go back upstairs.
PTE CORKHILL	*(Quietly calling)* I'm thirsty too, Sister.

SN Guilford goes to get his drink.

PTE CORKHILL	*(Quietly)* 'Climb the pyramid, I dare ya.' Got nowhere near the top, be dead if I did.

Returning, STAFF NURSE GUILFORD gives PRIVATE CORKHILL an injection in his thigh and a drink.

Thank you. *(The morphia slowly takes hold)* I'm going home aren't I? Finished before I even started. Don't think I can face 'em back home.

PRIVATE CORKHILL begins to struggle out of bed.

SN GUILFORD	You must stay in bed.

VD PATIENT stands at the ward door in the shadows — he smokes.

PTE CORKHILL	I haven't been anywhere but here and my home. Seen nothing. Done nothing. You can't send me home like this.

PRIVATE Corkhill clutches at her hand as he finally succumbs to sleep.

STAFF NURSE GUILFORD sees the VD PATIENT at the door.

VD PATIENT	Can I have something to drink?
SN GUILFORD	*(Quietly)* You must go back to your bed.

VD PATIENT   The orderly's not there.

SN GUILFORD   Oh, we'll find him. The best thing for you is rest. And you should put out that cigarette.

STAFF NURSE GUILFORD exits, taking her lantern.

There is a sound of a scuffle, STAFF NURSE GUILFORD's stifled scream and the lantern hitting the floor. It goes out.

ACT TWO | SCENE 3

Nurses' quarters, 2AGH, Mena House, CAIRO, EGYPT.

3am, 28 March 1915.

FLO sits in her room unable to sleep. She writes home for the first time.

FLO   28th of March, 1915. Mena House, Cairo.
                       To All At Home, I have been very busy since
                       my departure and have only just had the
                       chance to write. *(She stops writing)* I have
                       received no letters from you. *(She resumes
                       writing)* All is well with me. I trust Daisy's
                       wedding went well. Let me know how it went.
                       Did Granny stay awake? Did Uncle —

*FLO picks up the letter and crumples it. STAFF NURSE GUILFORD,
with no apron and holding her veil, comes into the room and begins
searching through her trunk. FLO quickly puts the crumpled letter in her
apron pocket.*

                       What are you looking for?

SN GUILFORD   Nothing, I just wanted to — to — why aren't
                       you asleep?

FLO   Can't it wait?

*STAFF NURSE GUILFORD finds her iron and proceeds to iron her
crumpled veil.*

SN GUILFORD   I just need to get this done.

FLO   Are all the patients asleep?

SN GUILFORD   I think so.

FLO   Where's your apron?

SN GUILFORD   ... I'm not sure.

FLO   The iron needs to be hot.

STAFF NURSE GUILFORD looks for her spare apron.

	Now what? April, go back to the wards.
SN GUILFORD	I am just — I need an apron.
FLO	Well hurry up.
SN GUILFORD	I will I will, I just need to find a clean one — here, got it.

STAFF NURSE GUILFORD begins to iron her apron now.

FLO	It doesn't need ironing. Just go or I'll tell Miss Watson you're not on the wards.
SN GUILFORD	A difficult patient.
FLO	What?
SN GUILFORD	I shouldn't have let go.
FLO	April, you need to go back to the wards —
SN GUILFORD	No one will notice!
FLO	Just do your work.
SN GUILFORD	Why don't you like me?
FLO	What? I'm tired, go back to the ward, and get the orderly. He can help you.
SN GUILFORD	He's not there.
FLO	Well he should be.
SN GUILFORD	Well he's not.
FLO	Deal with the patient yourself.
SN GUILFORD	I shouldn't have let go of his hand.
FLO	Whose hand?

MATRON WATSON enters.

MATRON WATSON   Sister Guilford, you're here. You must go back to the wards.

SN GUILFORD   I...

MATRON WATSON   Are you sick?

SN GUILFORD   No, Miss Watson, I just need to — I needed a clean apron.

MATRON WATSON   Well you have it now, so off you go.

Silence.

Sister Guilford, I said go back to the wards.

STAFF NURSE GUILFORD starts to fix her hair and put on her veil.

Are you ill?

SN GUILFORD   I'm going back.

STAFF NURSE GUILFORD goes to leave but stops then goes over to her kit to look for something else.

I just need to find... I don't seem to —

MATRON WATSON   Is something the matter?

FLO   A difficult patient.

MATRON WATSON   Well, I am sorry but you will have to learn to deal with him. If a patient is being difficult, it's usually for a reason. It can't be easy for them.

SN GUILFORD   I just need to find...

MATRON WATSON   No, stop that, go back to your wards now.

SN GUILFORD   The men are asleep.

MATRON WATSON   You cannot leave your wards unattended for any reason. Go back with me now or I will report you.

SN GUILFORD	No.
MATRON WATSON	I beg your pardon?
SN GUILFORD	No.
MATRON WATSON	I will have you returned home for dereliction of duty. Do you understand?
FLO	April, don't be stupid.
SN GUILFORD	I'm unfit for the job.
MATRON WATSON	*(To FLO)* Can you leave the room, please?

FLO exits.

	Well?
SN GUILFORD	Send me home.
MATRON WATSON	I see. I'll have to make a report. Headquarters will want to know why.
SN GUILFORD	As I said, I'm unfit for the job.
MATRON WATSON	You're not unfit for the job. I've seen your work.
SN GUILFORD	I'd like to go home.

Silence.

MATRON WATSON	You're throwing away your career. You refuse to go back?

SISTER GUILFORD nods yes.

	I will have to have you taken down to the holding cells.
SN GUILFORD	I need to bathe.

ACT TWO | SCENE 4

Nurses' quarters, 2AGH, Mena House, CAIRO, EGYPT.

7.55am, 28 March 1915.

MATRON WATSON	Are these all of Guilford's possessions?
FLO	Yes.

MATRON WATSON begins to pack Guilford's kit.

MATRON WATSON	Your Movement Orders are in. British unit. The hospital ship *Gascon*.
FLO	Another ship.
MATRON WATSON	Yes.
FLO	And you?
MATRON WATSON	I'm staying here.
FLO	Is April going home?
MATRON WATSON	Yes.
FLO	Can I do that, Miss?
MATRON WATSON	No, she asked me to do it.
FLO	Does she know that our orders are in? *(Matron Watson nods yes)* But surely a new place, new —
MATRON WATSON	It's out of our hands. Headquarters have been notified.
FLO	What will happen to her?

MATRON WATSON   Well, she won't nurse again, not for the army.
                       It is not the first time I have seen something
                       like this happen and I doubt it will be the last.

FLO   Something like what?

Silence.

MATRON WATSON   She is a good nurse. You are a good nurse.

                       I saw from your file that it was
                       your birthday last week.

*MATRON WATSON secures Guilford's possessions. She takes the
suitcase off, leaving FLO alone. FLO takes the crumpled letter from
her apron packet and smooths it out. She sits down to write...*

Barge with wounded alongside the hospital ship *Gascon*.
Photograph taken by Sister Alice Joan Twynam.

Australian War Memorial, A02740.

ACT THREE | SCENE 1

Aboard the British hospital ship Gascon, *off the coast of TURKEY.*

1am, 25 April 1915.

MAJOR JAMES FORREST, a British officer, stands on deck. He has a pipe but is unable to smoke it. The only sound is water gently lapping the hull. The ship is in complete blackout. A thin moon illuminates the sky.

FLO and a British nurse, SISTER HILDA SMITH, chat quietly.

SISTER SMITH	What do you call tea?
FLO	Tea.
SISTER SMITH	Oh. I just love your accent.
FLO	You're from the North aren't you?
SISTER SMITH	Yes, how'd you guess? York, just outside it, really.
FLO	My father was born near York. Thank goodness the sea is calm.
SISTER SMITH	Don't you like ships?
FLO	No.
SISTER SMITH	Why'd your father leave York?
FLO	To make his fortune, he's an engineer. Steel. He's manager of a factory now. He makes bayonets.
MAJOR FORREST	*(Quietly)* Can't sleep, Sisters?
SISTER SMITH	It's a bit airless in the cabins, Major.
MAJOR FORREST	Yes... *(A very faint rattle of a plate or cup dropping from the distant hills is heard)* Listen... *(All are silent. A distant donkey brays)* The fools should be quieter. We shouldn't be out here talking. Go back to your cabins, try to get some sleep.

SISTER SMITH	We will. Good night, Major.
FLO	Night, Major Forrest.

They all exit back to their cabins. Aboard the Gascon, *MAJOR FORREST waits until he is below deck before lighting his pipe, he paces the corridor before exiting.*

Small lanterns and candles flicker on one by one across the stage as the participants in the campaign begin to write down their thoughts and impressions, in letters home, in journals, on scraps of paper. They speak quietly as they write.

Aboard the Gascon, *FLO prepares her uniform and tidies her cabin and takes out a letter and reads it and looks at the photo enclosed within it. SISTER SMITH takes out a photo of her son. ORDERLY BARRIE shaves in his cabin. MATRON SIMCOX walks the corridors taking stock of the preparations on board.*

Elsewhere, on a nearby troopship, LT DAVIES is unable to sleep in his cabin. On the slopes of Ari Burnu, YILMAZ sits in his dugout by candle light. CAPITAINE CAGNET lies on his cot in a French hospital ship.

SISTER SMITH	It's just after one in the morning, can't sleep, so I shall continue my ramble.
ORDERLY BARRIE	James, you'll be glad to hear that we are finally going to see some action.
SISTER SMITH	The new Australian Sisters are very friendly, I find it rather refreshing but Miss Simcox is not fond of them, she doesn't approve of their wearing scarlet capes.
ORDERLY BARRIE	Wish I was out there with the fighting men. Will do all I can for them here.
SISTER SMITH	I was glad to receive a letter from Lady Forsyth, and the Edgwares send me parcels quite often.
ORDERLY BARRIE	Home is not far from my mind. Tell Mother I am in God's hands and am happy to be.

SISTER SMITH   The last one dated 18th April so they are still
                        getting through despite several ships going
                        down and lives and letters lost.

ORDERLY BARRIE   It is an exciting time and I am glad to
                        bear witness.

SISTER SMITH   We're lucky to receive any really.

SISTER SMITH stops writing and kneels by her bunk to pray.

ORDERLY BARRIE   I shall try to write down all I see before our
                        men take Constantinople.

MATRON SIMCOX   *(Writing in unit ledger)* One a.m.
                        No disturbances. Clear, calm conditions.
                        Wards prepared.

ORDERLY BARRIE   Your loving brother, Owen.

ORDERLY BARRIE sleeps.

MATRON SIMCOX   *(Signs ledger)* Miss Simcox. April 25th, 1915.

MATRON SIMCOX checks over the ledger silently.

LT DAVIES   *(Writing in his journal)* I see it all unfold. I
                        stand at the bow of the lighter, all in silence,
                        and about us battleships and destroyers float,
                        dimly discernible in the thin moonlight. In
                        front, the precipitous cliffs are dark against
                        the sky. The word of command comes, we
                        push off — almost immediately the cliffs
                        and scrub awake with the crack of rifles
                        and artillery. Flashes of light. The bullets of
                        the enemy plop into the water like pebbles.
                        I laugh. At the oars, strong men bend their
                        backs as we glide towards the beach. As we
                        get nearer, the aim of the Turks becomes
                        truer. Rifle and shrapnel bullets ziff past,

whispering in my ears. Ziff, ziff, death.
Machine guns on the left flank open out, and
a hail of lead whistles around us. The boat
crunches into the beach, the water is cold.
The bullets still miss, one strikes a pebble and
jumps up to bite me, and I feel blood trickling
down my face.

YILMAZ ONBAŞI   *(Corporal, writing a letter, in his trench —
speaking in Turkish)*
Beş askere can veren şanlı ana![1]

LT DAVIES   I turn to look back at my men,
they are all dead.

LIEUTENANT DAVIES waits for dawn.

YILMAZ ONBAŞI   *(Writing a letter — speaking in English, with
accent)* Glorious Turkish mother who gave
life to five soldiers! I have received your
letter while I am sitting in my earthen home.
Your letter encouraged my soul and I am
enraptured by the beauty of nature and wish
so much that I could share this beauty with
you. Every morning I am greeted by the
sunrise as I get up from my earth bedstead.
I approach the edge of the hole and, looking
out of it, catch the first rays of the warming
sun. The air is fresh. God gave this treasury
to the Turkish nation, for her, for you mother,
for Sevket, Mustafa, Huseyin and Bahadır.
I picked rosemary. I am enclosing it as a
souvenir of Gelibolu.

---

1   Phonetically, Besh askere juhn veren shanluh ah-nah. (Glorious Turkish mother who
gave life to five soldiers!)

CNE CAGNET   *(Doctor, writing in his journal — speaking in*
                     French) Le crépuscule de ce jour du 24
                     est passé...[2]

YILMAZ ONBAŞI   The sun will soon be rising on this spring
                     day. *(In Turkish)* Allah seni korusun.[3]
                     (In English) Your son, Nasir.

Yilmaz Onbaşı moves along the trench and out of sight.

CNE CAGNET   *(Speaking in English, with accent)* The twilight
                     of this day of the 24th has passed and we
                     wait until the first light of dawn, when we
                     will no doubt look upon our injured in an
                     atmosphere of blood and unspeakable horror.
                     How much will this little piece of earth cost?

He paces and smokes, exiting into the dark corridors. Darkness descends
as all but a few finally rest.

FLO   You have written to me. Our letters
                     crossed without knowing it. You have
                     forgiven me. *(She holds up a wedding*
                     photo of the family) My sister is an angel.
                     Do you see how beautiful you all look?
                     Write again and again and I will too.
                     I miss you all so much. I am sorry.

She stands and waits for morning.

---

2   Phonetically, Lur cre-poo-scool do seh-jour do van-katr eh pas-eh. (The twilight of
this day of the 24th has passed.)
3   Phonetically, Ah-llah seh-ni kor-soon. (God bless you.)

ACT THREE | SCENE 2

Aboard the British hospital ship Gascon *off the coast of TURKEY.*

Just before dawn, 25 April 1915.

FLO is below deck in her cabin as dawn breaks.

FLO	*(Singing quietly)* On this little gray ship going west.

Rifle fire is heard echoing across the bay — artillery starts up. All on board the Gascon *are jolted awake. FLO, SISTER SMITH and MATRON SIMCOX rush onto deck to stand witness to the troop landings.*

April 25th. Red letter day. It has begun.

A shell lands in the water close to the ship clearing the deck, sending the nurses back from the rails. Several lighters carrying wounded can be heard approaching over the distant attacks. The sound of wounded spilling into the space becomes louder and louder.

ACTORS deliver the following lines standing still. [4]

MAJOR FORREST	Set him down there.
	(To FLO about PATIENT A) Check pulse and blood pressure. Get him warm, he's clammy to the touch.
	(To SMITH about PATIENT B) Put him over there. What's his tag say?
SISTER SMITH	Shattered humerus.
PATIENT B	I'll be right, there's worse off outside.

---

4   This scene was known as 'rolling wounded' in the original productions. Three stretchers were used, with actors 5 and 6 playing multiple roles as patients and orderlies until, by the end of the scene, all patients were imagined. The soundscape is as described in LT DAVIES' journal (Act Three, Scene 1) but reflects the distance of the hospital ship from the shore. The sound intensifies throughout the scene.

MAJOR FORREST	*(To FLO about PATIENT A)* Not just blankets — hot water bottles. What's his pulse?
FLO	Quite rapid.
MATRON SIMCOX	*(At door)* Sister Smith, can you help me?

ACTORS rush into action.

MATRON SIMCOX rushes to the exit. FLO and MAJOR FORREST attend to PATIENT A. SISTER SMITH attends to PATIENT B.

MAJOR FORREST	*(To SMITH about PATIENT B)* Leave him.
	(To FLO about PATIENT A) He'll need to warm up before I can do anything.
	(To SMITH) Sister Smith, help Miss Simcox.

SISTER SMITH leaves PATIENT B and exits.

> *(To FLO about PATIENT A)* His arm is pulped. Give him some morphia, put a sling on it and then get him to surgery.

MAJOR FORREST attends to PATIENT C who has been sitting quietly. FLO prepares the morphia, injects PATIENT A.

> *(About PATIENT C)* Forearm gutter, I'll deal with this.
>
> *(To FLO about PATIENT A)* Hurry up.

FLO leaves PATIENT A to make room for SISTER SMITH and MATRON SIMCOX as they bring in a heavily-laden stretcher that will soon hold PATIENT D.

After putting the stretcher down, SISTER SMITH moves to check on PATIENT A. MATRON SIMCOX moves to help FLO lead PATIENT B out, who transforms into PATIENT D and lies on stretcher left for him.

MAJOR FORREST   *(To SMITH about PATIENT A)* Leave him!

(To FLO about PATIENT D) What is it?

FLO   *(Checking tag of PATIENT D)* Jaw, Major.

MAJOR FORREST   *(To SISTER SMITH about PATIENT C)* Come here, tie that off, I need to move on.

SISTER SMITH   But, Sir — I —

MATRON SIMCOX   You can't expect —

MAJOR FORREST   Just do it, Smith.

MATRON SIMCOX and SISTER SMITH attend to PATIENT C.

(To FLO about PATIENT D) Get those filthy dressings off. *(Removal of bandages sees PATIENT D bleed out)* Put pressure there.

(To MATRON SIMCOX) Blood bucket, Miss Simcox.

SISTER SMITH ties the end of PATIENT C's suture the best she can. MATRON SIMCOX exits. MAJOR FORREST throws bloodied bandages onto the floor as MATRON SIMCOX returns with a bucket.

MATRON SIMCOX   In the bucket please, Major.

MATRON SIMCOX gives blood bucket to FLO. MAJOR FORREST throws bloodied bandages and waste into the bucket.

SISTER SMITH leads PATIENT C off — he becomes PATIENT E. SISTER SMITH returns, struggling to support PATIENT E as he has a broken ankle. MATRON SIMCOX moves to help SISTER SMITH.

MATRON SIMCOX   Broken ankle, Major.

MAJOR FORREST   He'll have to wait. No, get him out of here. We are supposed to be dealing with bullet wounds. Perforating and penetrating wounds only.

*MATRON SIMCOX and SISTER SMITH reluctantly help PATIENT E
to the exit. SISTER SMITH returns with MATRON SIMCOX carrying in
PATIENT F (imagined) on a stretcher.*

SISTER SMITH   *(To PATIENT F)* It'll be alright, son. Stay with
                                me. He's bleeding heavily, it won't stop, right
                                through the bandage, sir. It won't stop.

MAJOR FORREST   *(To SISTER SMITH about PATIENT F)*
                                Alright, Smith. Apply pressure.

*FLO and MAJOR FORREST work to pack the missing jaw of PATIENT
D. SISTER SMITH works on PATIENT F. MATRON SIMCOX exits.*

                                (To FLO about PATIENT D) That'll have to
                                do.

                                Tidy it up.

MAJOR FORREST joins SISTER SMITH to help with PATIENT F.

                                (To SISTER SMITH about PATIENT F)
                                Make that tight. *(To FLO about PATIENT D)*
                                Finished? Take him out to the wards. *(To
                                SISTER SMITH about PATIENT F)* Tighter!
                                Get him to surgical as soon as possible.

*FLO attempts to help PATIENT D to his feet. SISTER SMITH continues
to pack PATIENT F's abdomen with lint.*

FLO   He's too heavy for me.

MAJOR FORREST   Orderly!

ORDERLY #1 enters.

                                *(To ORDERLEY #1 about FLO about
                                PATIENT D)* Take him to the wards.

ORDERLY #1 helps PATIENT D off the stretcher and walks him out.

FLO stands somewhat at a loss for the briefest of moments.

MATRON SIMCOX   *(off)* Sister Whiting!

FLO exits and re-enters with MATRON SIMCOX who leads in PATIENT G (imagined) on a stretcher.

FLO   Chest.

MAJOR FORREST leaves SISTER SMITH with PATIENT F and joins FLO to attend to PATIENT G.

MAJOR FORREST   *(To FLO about PATIENT G)* Fetch more
                               packing lint.

FLO slips on bloody floor.

                               (To FLO) Get up!

ORDERLY #1 and ORDERLY #2 enter with PATIENT H (imagined) on a stretcher.

ORDERLY #1   *(about PATIENT H)* Head wound, Major.

MAJOR FORREST   *(about PATIENT H)* He's blue, put him there.

                               It'll have to wait.

ORDERLY #1 and ORDERLY #2 place PATIENT H stretcher down and head towards the exit.

SISTER SMITH   Orderlies!

ORDERLY #1 and ORDERLY #2 then assist SISTER SMITH and take PATIENT F on a stretcher and exit. SISTER SMITH moves to PATIENT A but it's useless and she stumbles away from him.

Led in by MATRON SIMCOX, ORDERLY #1 and ORDERLY #2 bring in PATIENT I (imagined) on a stretcher.

MATRON SIMCOX   Penetrating shoulder.

MAJOR FORREST   *(To MATRON SIMCOX)* Over there.

ORDERLY #1 and ORDERLY #2 place PATIENT I on stretcher on the ground and move to exit — they have difficulty navigating the maze of stretchers.

SISTER SMITH attends to PATIENT I.

(To SMITH about PATIENT I) Flush it out and bandage it — that's all.

SISTER SMITH gets irrigation syringe and bandages from medical box and returns to treat PATIENT I.

(To MATRON SIMCOX) Empty that, Matron.

MATRON SIMCOX takes blood bucket and exits. As the ORDERLIES are about to exit —

MAJOR FORREST   *(To ORDERLIES about PATIENT G)* Wait, I'm done, take him out.

ORDERLY #1 and ORDERLY #2 exit with PATIENT G on a stretcher.

MAJOR FORREST moves to assist SISTER SMITH with PATIENT I, and notices PATIENT H is lifeless.

(To FLO about PATIENT H) Take his pulse.

FLO attends to PATIENT H. SISTER SMITH moves to medical box to get more bandages.

FLO   I can't find it.

MAJOR FORREST   *(Moves to assist FLO about PATIENT H)* That's because he's dead.

Orderlies!

ORDERLY #1 and ORDERLY #2 enter.

Take him to the morgue.

ORDERLY #1 and ORDERLY #2 exit with PATIENT H on stretcher, re-enter immediately with PATIENT J.

MATRON SIMCOX   *(PATIENT J)* Neck, entry and exit.

MAJOR FORREST   *(To SMITH about PATIENT I)* That man is being sick.

SISTER SMITH rushes to help PATIENT I.

FLO is forgetting to breathe. She stands.

The whole cycle is repeated around FLO in silence with only the sound of battle audible. The action gets faster but soon exhaustion sets in, days are felt to pass.

FLO is moving through the action, helping where she can, slowly moving towards the ship's rails. We hear the sound of seagulls and the ship at full steam.

CHAPLAIN   *(Off)* We therefore commit their bodies to the deep, looking for the general Resurrection in the last day, and the life of the world to come, through our Lord Jesus Christ.

On deck, SISTER SMITH and ORDERLY #1 and ORDERLY #2 lift the end of their stretchers one by one to allow a body (imagined) to slide into the sea. We hear the bodies slide and splash into the ocean.

FLO   Bury me on land. My land.

Placing the stretchers back down, SISTER SMITH, FLO and ORDERLY #1 and ORDERLY #2 exit.

INTERVAL *or* CONTINUE

Sisters at No. 3 Australian General Hospital on the island of Lemnos. Tented wards flank a road through the hospital.

Photo: A.W. Savage. Mitchell Library, State Library of NSW, PXE 698.

ACT FOUR | SCENE 1

Mudros Harbour, LEMNOS, GREECE.

8pm, 7 August 1915.

Blazing sunset at the end of a hot dusty day. Insects swarm among the large group of nursing staff of the 3rd Australian General Hospital who gather on a makeshift jetty.

SISTER DOUGLAS sits on a pile of crates with her kit bag, swatting endless bugs away.

SISTER DOUGLAS	What ship were you on?
FLO	*(Turning)* Mary?
SISTER DOUGLAS	*(They hug)* Oh I have missed you! Don't ask me why, but I have. We're together again Flo, and a new home! *(Surveying the ground)* Mind you, it's not looking promising is it? I think the ground is alive...
FLO	I would kiss the ground, if I could stop swaying. No more ships. Ever. I will walk home. I have never been so happy to have little bugs crawling all over me. Mind you, that one's not so little, what is that?

They jump onto nearby crates to get off the ground.

SISTER DOUGLAS	Who knows — leave it — it could bite. Yes, no ships for Flo! And I will never look at a merry-go-round again.
FLO	Merry-go-round?
SISTER DOUGLAS	Heliopolis. We ran out of space, so we took over Luna Park. All of it. Merry-go-round, the rink — I treated men in the ghost train... skeletal men staring at painted skeletons on the walls... But enough. I have my Flo back.

FLO	And I have my Mary.
SISTER DOUGLAS	My Mary? I wonder how Harry and Stanley are getting on… Let's not think of it, let's think of something else… something luxurious — a deep, hot bath and champagne.
FLO	Breakfast in bed and fresh white sheets.
SISTER DOUGLAS	Strawberry jam, mum's scones.
FLO	Butter and fresh bread.
SISTER DOUGLAS	Real tea.
FLO	Real milk.
SISTER DOUGLAS	Lipstick.
FLO	Lipstick?
SISTER DOUGLAS	My last lipstick melted in the Cairo heat. Nothing to leave the boys with an impression of me.
FLO	Sister Mary Douglas.
SISTER DOUGLAS	Woman cannot live by bread alone.

MATRON WATSON enters, she has been walking.

MATRON WATSON	Sorry Sisters, there's no one around as far as I can see. I'm sure they know we're here and someone will be down to greet us.
FLO	I'm just glad to be on solid ground.
MATRON WATSON	Yes, I remember, that's right. It's so good to have us all back together again. Are you both well?
SISTER DOUGLAS	Yes, Miss Watson, thank you.
FLO	Yes, Miss. And you?
MATRON WATSON	I'm good, yes. Now, are you two going to behave this time?

BAGPIPE PLAYER starts to play — ear-splittingly loud — then stops.

Well the piper is here. That must
mean something.

COLONEL FRANCES enters.

Ah, this must be Colonel Frances. Now —

COL FRANCES   Evening ladies. We must be on our way.
Form fours.

MATRON WATSON   Sorry Colonel, form fours?

COL FRANCES   *(Slower, clearer)* Form fours.

MATRON WATSON   You mean formation? No need of that
Colonel, we can all just walk together. We're
all tired and would like to get to our quarters.
So, lead the way.

COL FRANCES   Miss Watson, we have a two mile march to
the hospital site, some formation and order is
required. We cannot have you wandering the
island... just form two orderly lines. That's it,
ladies, line up. Right, so we shall march...

The 3rd Australian General Hospital
welcomes the nursing sisters to Lemnos.

*Nods to the BAGPIPE PLAYER who blasts into a traditional
marching song.*

Now march!

It would be easier, ladies, if you march in
time. That's right, think of it as a dance.
There we go, well done. Let's get there before
sunrise.

The sun sets.

ACT FOUR | SCENE 2

Tented ward, 3AGH, TURKS HEAD, LEMNOS, GREECE.

11pm, 7 August 1915.

A tented ward that has no side walls. The tent is lit by a lantern.

PATIENT #2 and LIEUTENANT DAVIES sit on the bare ground or on a crate. PATIENT #2 is from New Zealand. He has a head wound and his left hand is clearly missing under an extensive bandage. He is in immense amounts of pain. He uses a bed pan as a pillow. LT DAVIES is suffering from fever and is vomiting — bile, then dry retching. He has been using his helmet as a bucket.

SISTER DOUGLAS and FLO approach.

FLO	No rest for the wicked.
SISTER DOUGLAS	Let's hope the wards are better than our 'tents'.

The Sisters are shocked at the condition of the ward.

PATIENT #2	Can you get that man a bucket, Sister? His helmet appears to be full.
FLO	I'll get it.
LT DAVIES	Wait, I need — *(He retches into the helmet)*
SISTER DOUGLAS	*(Checking PATIENT #2's bandages)* These are field dressings... hasn't anything been done for you?
PATIENT #2	They pointed to the ground and said 'sit'. That was yesterday.
SISTER DOUGLAS	These have to come off now.
PATIENT #2	Heard that before.
LT DAVIES	*(To FLO)* You look familiar.
FLO	We all look familiar, Lieutenant.

Banging into a tent pole in the dark, PATIENT #1 enters having used the facilities. He has a severe head wound. He is English. He also has the trots.

PATIENT #1 — Dark 'ol night. Clearly the latrines were built by the enemy — taken better shits in a —

PATIENT #2 — Mind ya language! We've an officer in our midst.

PATIENT #1 — And so we do, beg yours, Lieutenant. *(To FLO and SISTER DOUGLAS)* Hello! Delicate types these officers — aren't they Sisters?

SISTER DOUGLAS — *(To PATIENT #1)* You mustn't go to the latrines unassisted. It's dangerous, you could collapse. Fall in.

PATIENT #1 — You're not wrong.

LT DAVIES — May I have some water, Sister?

FLO goes to leave but MATRON WATSON enters.

FLO — Miss Watson.

MATRON WATSON — Sisters.

PATIENT #1 — Sorry Matron, if I'd have known we were having more visitors, I'd have got the lads to put up some more walls. Sit down, pull up a helmet.

PATIENT #2 — Not that one.

FLO — *(Quietly)* There's no supplies or anything really, Miss. I was just going to get some water —

MATRON WATSON — *(To SISTER DOUGLAS)* Go and get some spare aprons and petticoats, there are several in my kit.

SISTER DOUGLAS exits.

> When she gets back, cut them into bandages.
> I'll look for water. And I'll take that helmet.
> *(She takes Davies' helmet. Indicating a*
> *scorpion on the ground)* See to that scorpion.

MATRON WATSON exits.

FLO kicks the scorpion out of the tent, it takes her several tries.

PATIENT #2	Believe she's just invented a new sport.
PATIENT #1	That was very graceful.

FLO smiles.

	There we are lads, we have a smile!
PATIENT #2	Feeling better already. Who needs medicine?

SISTER DOUGLAS re-enters carrying aprons and petticoats which she is already tearing into strips.

SISTER DOUGLAS	Got them.
FLO	Matron said to cut them into bandages.
SISTER DOUGLAS	Thought of that already.
PATIENT #1	Petticoat bandages. You gotta laugh really.
SISTER DOUGLAS	None of this is remotely funny. Now, where are my scissors?!
PATIENT #2	Lighten up, Sister.
PATIENT #1	No son, she's right. You've lost your left hand, I've lost half me brain, she's lost her scissors — *(Lt Davies retches)* he's lost his lunch. What's to laugh at?
PATIENT #2	Lucky I'm right-handed.

All laugh.

MATRON WATSON enters with a cup of water.

MATRON WATSON   That's the way Sisters, keep their spirits up.

MATRON WATSON hands LT DAVIES the cup, he drinks greedily.

Slowly.

LT DAVIES vomits and MATRON WATSON catches it in her hands.

Forgot the bucket.

MATRON WATSON exits, cupping the vomit in her hands.

LT DAVIES   Cut hand…

FLO   No it's not.

LT DAVIES   In Cairo… I never forget a smile.

PATIENT #2   This guy is smooth.

LT DAVIES   Davies, Lieutenant William Davies.

Can I take you to see the pyramids?

FLO   Pyramids? *(FLO remembers him now)*

PATIENT #2   Oh, he's delirious. Mate, we're in Greece. Lemnos.

Officers — wouldn't know the
ass end of a donkey.

LT DAVIES   Or the Sphinx.

FLO catches LT DAVIES as he collapses.

FLO   Just rest.

Do you like books? I have a few with me. I
can read one to you.

SISTER DOUGLAS Well isn't this romantic. Have you all been checked for lice?

PATIENT #1 Chats are the least of my worries. I need to use the facilities...

SISTER DOUGLAS Use the bedpan. *(Reaches for Patient #2's 'pillow')*

PATIENT #1 Not on your life.

PATIENT #1 exits. SISTER DOUGLAS calls after him.

SISTER DOUGLAS You can't go alone, it's dark.

MATRON WATSON returns with a plate of biscuits and a bucket.

MATRON WATSON Found some food of sorts. Hard tack.

LT DAVIES retches. MATRON WATSON thrusts bucket towards him.

  No, no, in the bucket.

PATIENT #2 Scorpion.

MATRON WATSON Where?

FLO stamps on it. The tent falls down around them.

ACT FOUR | SCENE 3

Tented ward, 3AGH, TURKS HEAD, LEMNOS, GREECE.

Morning, 10 September 1915.

FLO	You're dressed?
LT DAVIES	We're moving on soon… not sure… a day or two — I feel much stronger today, even ready for exercise. More than just our strolls around the grounds.
FLO	Alright, how about I organise an orderly to take you —
LT DAVIES	Yes, walking is good. Anyway you probably need to get to wherever you're supposed to be…
FLO	I'm on duty. This is where I'm supposed to be.
LT DAVIES	Of course, yes… is there any chance of a cup of tea?
FLO	Yes, I'll go and — *(She goes to leave)*
LT DAVIES	No, no, I'm sorry. I meant that one of the orderlies could go and get me…
FLO	I'll go and get your tea, Lieutenant. *(She goes to leave)*
LT DAVIES	Would you like to go for a walk this evening, Sister? Not far, just down to the harbour. I probably couldn't handle much more anyway… You can bring another Sister if you like. Or we can organise a group — you don't have to if you don't want to, just thought… get out for some fresh air and scenery and you know, get the legs moving…

FLO

Alright.

LT DAVIES

Alright. Great. That's great. As a group or just you and... or just we two?

FLO

Just 'we two' is fine.

ACT FOUR | SCENE 4

Interior of COLONEL FRANCES' tent, 3AGH.
TURKS HEAD, LEMNOS, GREECE.

Mid-afternoon, 10 September 1915.

A gramophone sits on COLONEL FRANCES' desk. It plays a
classical tune ('Samson et Delilah' by Saint-Saens). A BATMAN
enters with a tray with a box of cigars, a decanter of whiskey
and a glass, setting them down. He salutes and exits.

COLONEL FRANCES pours himself a glass.

MATRON WATSON	*(A knock at the tent frame)* Excuse me, Colonel.
COL FRANCES	Miss Watson, I don't have time at the moment.
MATRON WATSON	You've been busy every time I have tried.
COL FRANCES	Yes, Miss Watson, there is a war on.
MATRON WATSON	Are you aware how desperate the situation is getting? The facilities must be brought up to standard.
COL FRANCES	I am aware, Matron.
MATRON WATSON	There are barely enough medical supplies. We need access to better food and cleaner water. And the nurses' quarters must be completed. I am concerned, as we progress towards winter, half the hospital will be unable to function — no one will be well enough to work.

COL FRANCES   I have seen the conditions, I am aware of the shortages. I'm as appalled as you are — the conditions here are among the worst I've encountered. Numerous requests for supplies have been made to Headquarters, only to be told the ships have been delayed, gone down, been redirected. We are at war. Sacrifices need to be made by everyone.

MATRON WATSON   From where I stand it appears that the patients and nurses are the ones who are making those sacrifices.

COL FRANCES   I am aware your nurses are struggling in the harsh conditions. I'm sorry, I don't like to see women in distress, but what did you expect?

MATRON WATSON   What did I expect?

COL FRANCES   Your nurses are struggling because of their lack of suitability for the realities of war. They are unaccustomed to army life and have been found wanting. We cannot make special allowances for your staff. We have a job to do and it must be done.

MATRON WATSON   Colonel Frances, this is not about the suitability —

COL FRANCES   Miss Watson, I have two young daughters. I shudder at the thought of them ever going through what you ladies have been through, but thankfully they are not of that bent. Some people do not have the backbone for war.

MATRON WATSON   Backbone?

My nurses have not been found wanting. The facilities have been found wanting; the army's chain of supply has been found wanting. The nurses do not need special allowances. The working conditions are sub —

COL FRANCES   Which you women seem unable to adapt to —

MATRON WATSON   How are they not adapting? The nurses have
                     risen to every challenge, endlessly adapting.
                     The wounded are thankful for their presence,
                     for their compassion, their empathy.

COL FRANCES   Compassion and empathy get short
                     shrift during wartime. It is back
                     home where the women of our
                     country are doing the most good.

MATRON WATSON   I beg your pardon?

COL FRANCES   I see it wherever I go, Matron. When women
                     are thrust upon men, they cause havoc and
                     dissention. Men lose all judgment in the
                     presence of women. Temptation and vice
                     creep in and undermine discipline.

MATRON WATSON   Then the men must be more disciplined.

COL FRANCES   The men are here to work.

MATRON WATSON   We too are here to work.

COL FRANCES   To little or no benefit. You can't deny that
                     woman's great weakness is that she thrives off
                     the attentions of men — attention that should
                     be directed to the task at hand, not to the
                     waistline of a nurse. You are taking jobs from
                     the male orderlies, reducing them to mere
                     stretcher bearers and water carriers. We now
                     need four people to do the job of two.

MATRON WATSON   The male orderlies' duties have barely
                     changed. The nurses have training and skills
                     the orderlies do not possess.

COL FRANCES   When all is said and done you achieve little
                     more than helping the men recover a few
                     days faster. At what cost? Half of you will die
                     before the winter is out, as you said yourself.
                     You're too soft.

MATRON WATSON   What I have seen these women achieve —
and ask for nothing in return. The facilities
are not up to standard, Colonel, humane
standards and something must be done about
them.

You're a busy man, I can see that,
let me help you.

COL FRANCES   What can be done, has been done. I shall note
our meeting in the unit diary.

MATRON WATSON   Colonel.

Matron Watson exits.

COL FRANCES   Band of bloody bints.

ACT FOUR | SCENE 5

Exterior hillside, 3AGH. TURKS HEAD, LEMNOS, GREECE.

Sunset, 10 September 1915.

LIEUTENANT DAVIES is helped by BARNES. He builds a pyramid stack of bully beef boxes, then leads FLO in, her eyes covered.

FLO	Wait, where are you taking me?
LT DAVIES	Would you do me the honour of allowing me to escort you on a tour of the pyramids?
FLO	Pyramids?
LT DAVIES	It's a small pyramid — it won't take long.

He takes off her blindfold. They climb the stacked boxes.

	Worth the climb, no? The view from the top is spectacular.
FLO	Yes, I can see my tent.
LT DAVIES	My ward is just... the water purification unit... lovely harbour... x-ray...
	This is for you.
FLO	*(Overlapping)* I thought you —
LT DAVIES	No, after you.
FLO	I thought you might like — I didn't bring many books with me but this is one of my favourites *(Handing him the book, 'Robinson Crusoe')* — What were you going to say?
LT DAVIES	This is for you. *(Hands her a small Princess Mary tin)*
FLO	A Princess Mary tin...
LT DAVIES	Soon, I hope it'll be full.

FLO   With what?

LT DAVIES   Letters. From me. Can I write to you?

FLO   Could I stop you?

LT DAVIES   Unlikely. *(He descends the pyramid to look at the book)* Robinson Crusoe —

He opens the book and sees inscription from FLO's father inside —

                       'Happy 10th birthday, Flo.' When is your birthday?

FLO   March 1st.

LT DAVIES   Well then, you'll just have to be patient.

FLO   What for?

LT DAVIES   Your birthday kiss. May I — take a photo of you?

FLO   I suppose so.

LIEUTENANT DAVIES gets a pocket camera from his tunic and takes a photograph of FLO.

LT DAVIES   My orders are in. I leave tomorrow.

FLO   Sister Florence Whiting, care of the 3rd Australian General Hospital, Lemnos. That will reach me. Be safe.

LT DAVIES   Be good.

FLO   You be good.

LT DAVIES   You be safe.

ACT FOUR | SCENE 6

Interior tent, 3AGH. TURKS HEAD, LEMNOS, GREECE.

11pm, 28 October 1915.

FLO wears a balaclava, gloves, coat and clutches a hot water bottle.

FLO   *(Writes in her journal)*
                             October 28th, 1915, Lemnos.

                             Letters. Floods of letters after the drought.
                             Glorious words of love and comfort from
                             home. From him. From friends, from patients
                             I can't remember, from a few I can. I am
                             to be an Aunt. Life is normal. It can be. It
                             will be. I want it to be. This is my life. Dust
                             and blood. Blood red sunsets, wind, bugs
                             and pain. Black skin of frostbite, like rotted
                             leather. Bone. Old before my time. There are
                             so many sick staff... Mary has been bedridden
                             for three weeks. The doctors are dropping
                             like flies and the patients talk of an imminent
                             retreat. Miss Watson was re-assigned, no
                             idea where. No goodbyes, no chance to say
                             what she has come to mean to me, to all of
                             us. Colonel Frances is our matron now.

FLO sits silently writing.

*COLONEL FRANCES and an ANAESTHETIST (BARNES) wear
badly blood-stained surgical aprons under heavy coats. They struggle to
bring in a PATIENT on a stretcher. The patient (in a naval coal stoker's
uniform) has a bad abdominal wound.*

*BARNES puts the patient under. COLONEL FRANCES is feverish and
the symptoms of beriberi start to take hold.*

COL FRANCES   Is he under, Barnes? Where the hell is she? Let's get on with it before we all freeze to death. What are we dealing with here? He's filthy — and why is he soaking wet?

BARNES   This lot are off a torpedoed ship, Colonel.

COL FRANCES   Messy abdominal, how long was he in the water?

BARNES   Not sure.

COL FRANCES   *(Yelling off)* I need assistance here!

FLO enters.

     Finally, which one are you?

FLO   Sister Whiting, Colonel.

COL FRANCES   Don't stand there, move in.

FLO   I've never assisted in Surgical before, Colonel.

BARNES   There's no one else...

COL FRANCES   Let's get on with it. Come on, move in I say.

They proceed to operate.

FLO   He's soaking wet.

BARNES   Other side.

COLONEL FRANCES stumbles slightly as he pushes FLO away.

     Dangerous. Clean that mess up after this one is done. Apply pressure here and soak up the blood as I go.

Surgical removal of two pieces of shrapnel — they clang into the metal kidney bowl as they are removed. They work silently together for several minutes but the COLONEL stumbles again.

FLO	Are you all right, Colonel?
COL FRANCES	Get on with it, soak up the blood, I can't see a thing. You're in my light!

COLONEL FRANCES stumbles and his knees buckle.
FLO tries to stop him falling.

	Get off me!
FLO	Colonel, you're ill.
COL FRANCES	I'm aware of that.
	(To BARNES) Wake Major Richards.

BARNES exits.

COLONEL FRANCES moves aside.

COL FRANCES	There was a piece — I had it but it slipped — feel behind the gallbladder. There. Use your hands. *(FLO proceeds to gingerly feel around)* It was very small…

FLO finds one very small fragment.

	Got it?
FLO	*(Showing him her bloodied hand with a tiny fine piece of glinting metal on her fingertip)* I think so.
COL FRANCES	I need to — pack the abdomen. The cotton gauze is there. Lightly, no pressure, good, that's it. When Bar–
FLO	Can I do anything for you, Colonel?
COL FRANCES	It's beriberi.
FLO	Yes.

BARNES, running, re-enters.

BARNES   Major Richards is on his way.

COL FRANCES   Get him to x-ray —

COLONEL FRANCES exits.

BARNES   Welcome to surgical, Sister.

ACT FOUR | SCENE 7

Near a jetty, TURKS HEAD, LEMNOS, GREECE.

Mid-morning, 10 January 1916.

FLO stands alone on the shore. She watches the activity from the evacuation of the Gallipoli Peninsula and the shutting down of the Australian hospitals. She is dressed in her travel cape and carries her bag.

BARNES enters with a Red Cross Christmas billy.

BARNES	Found a spare Christmas billy. *(Hands it to FLO)*
FLO	Thank you. *(She doesn't open it)*
BARNES	You should join the others on the barge, you'll catch your death.
FLO	I will. How many men are we leaving behind on the Peninsula, do you think?
BARNES	Fair few. Where to next, you think? Cairo?
FLO	I'm hoping France.
BARNES	I was hoping Brisbane.
FLO	I'm going to miss this place.
BARNES	You women are mad! *(Exits)*

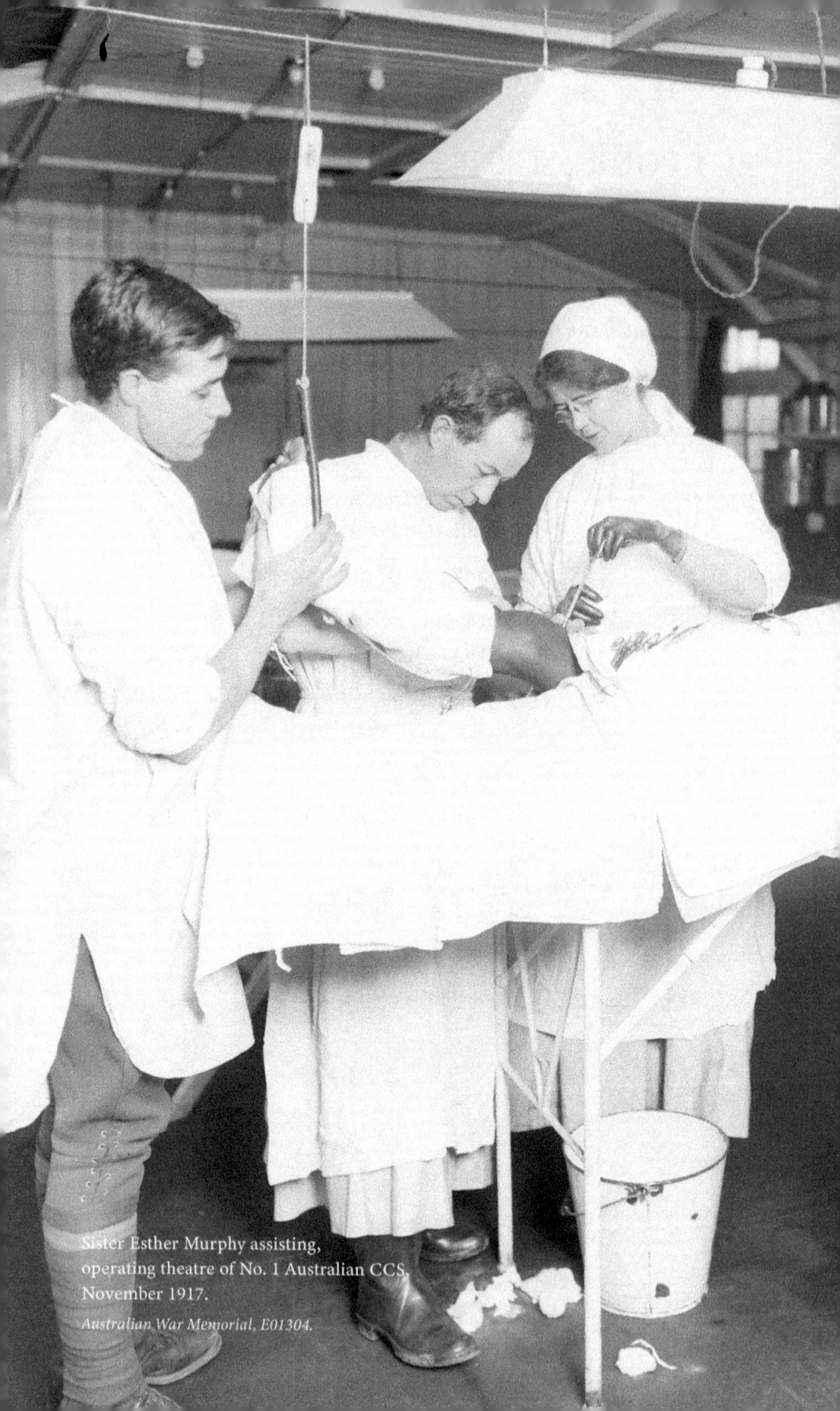

Sister Esther Murphy assisting,
operating theatre of No. 1 Australian CCS,
November 1917.

Australian War Memorial, E01304.

ACT FIVE | SCENE 1

Sisters' huts, 2nd Australian General Hospital, WIMEREUX, FRANCE.

11pm, 15 July 1916.

FLO stands at her hut door journal in hand, lit by lantern.
Canadian SISTER LAFFIN snores in her bed.

FLO   15th July, 1916, Wimereux.

                           Lemnos has left its mark. I've
                           found my place — assisting surgery.
                           Is it wrong to be proud?

SISTER LAFFIN snores.

                           And now summer in France…

                           Endless limbs and jaws and… too ghastly to
                           recall. The lingering stench of gangrene. This
                           Somme is hell. The world is at its own throat.

                           So hot again today. Assisted on 39 operations,
                           the day before 52, and before that 58…
                           Seven commanding officers in six months.
                           All getting younger.

                           My quarters here, a wooden hut with a
                           veranda. What will they be like in winter?
                           Hope not to still be here in winter.

SISTER LAFFIN snores.

                           Will Canada ever stop snoring?

                           I miss my Mary. I miss him. Where are they?
                           Miss Watson was sent to Rouen then Saint-
                           Omer, wherever they need her.

The WIMEREUX ORDERLY delivers letters to FLO.
One is from LIEUTENANT DAVIES — she opens and reads it;
a crumpled broken flower falls out to the floor.

LT DAVIES is seen sitting in his dugout writing a letter by candlelight.

LT DAVIES

Florence, I cannot tell you where I am but, from your recent letter, I can tell you I am not so far away at all. It brings me great comfort to think of you so close after all these months, and our frequent letters make up for that missed birthday kiss I owe you.

I have been promised leave in a few weeks' time. Can I come to you?

The flower I picked not far from here. I found it growing in the helmet of a fallen soldier. Will you believe me when I say it was a beautiful sight? A simple epitaph to mark the passing of his life. Keep it safe for him.

Pardon this scribbled note, I must go. But I cannot tell you how I long to see you, to hold you, to give you that kiss. Excuse my familiarity but our extended separation has brought clarity. William.

He takes the flower, places it in the envelope with his letter and tries to sleep. FLO puts flower and letter into her brass Princess Mary tin.

FLO

Come to me. The flower is beautiful. Florence.

FLO picks up a fountain pen and an unfinished letter.

Dear Mrs Haynes, I am writing to tell you of your son's last hours.

LT DAVIES writes another letter to FLO.

LT DAVIES   The stunts are endless and we have now been told that all leave is cancelled.

LIEUTENANT DAVIES turns away.

MR WHITING moves into the shadows and writes his letter to FLO.

MR WHITING   How are you, my girl? Another winter is upon us and you are still not home.

(A baby is heard)

We are all well. Daisy had the baby on the 1st of June, it was a good birth… I will leave those details to your mother's letter. It's a girl, she has called her Florence. Flossie. It's very cold here. We've even had a dusting of snow. The factory is steaming ahead for the war effort. If only it wasn't. I will write again soon. Father.

MR WHITING stands looking over his letter.

FLO   *(Finishing her letter to Mrs Haynes)* He was comfortable as I sat with him. He passed peacefully at dawn. Sister Florence Whiting.

FLO places Private Haynes' identity disk, taken from his body, into the envelope addressed to Mrs Haynes and closes it.

LT DAVIES   Two more of my unit killed today, mortar, instant. I had been standing in that spot a minute earlier but moved off to check another section of line. Can you remember my face?

FLO   *(Quietly)* I'm trying to.

ACT FIVE | SCENE 2

Open road, south of WIMEREUX, FRANCE.

Mid-November 1916.

FLO sits with SISTER LAFFIN on the back of an open army lorry, driven by a CANADIAN OFFICER. Australian troops can be heard calling out as the Sisters pass. The Sisters wave back in appreciation. The lorry rattles on slowly over muddy roads.

FLO	Well, Giggle, where are we off to?
SISTER LAFFIN	Stop calling me that.
FLO	Sister Laffin, laughing, giggling —
SISTER LAFFIN	It's just not that funny.
ANZAC SOLDIER	*(Calling — off)* I love you Sisters! Coo-eeee.
SISTER LAFFIN	And I love you!

Australian troops reply with wolf whistles, "Marry me!"

FLO	Giggle!
SISTER LAFFIN	They're Australian, say something Flo. It's an honour to make 'em happy!
	All the best boys!

More cat calls and cheers from the lads. FLO sees LIEUTENANT DAVIES and calls out.

FLO	William!

Troops can be heard calling "I'm William" — "No I'm William" — "I'm Bill" — "My middle name is William".

FLO jumps off the moving lorry as LT DAVIES sees her and runs towards her.

SISTER LAFFIN   Flo! *(Turning to OFFICER)* Stop, driver,
                     please stop!

FLO and LT DAVIES kiss. The troops go wild.

LT DAVIES   You do remember my face.

                     Happy birthday Flo. *(Kiss)* And that's for
                     my birthday. *(Kiss)* Easter. *(Kiss)* New Year's.
                     (Kiss)

                     We're back down the line for a night's leave.
                     I couldn't get news to you. *(Kiss)* That's for
                     last Christmas.

                     Can we go somewhere quiet?

CANADIAN OFFICER   Sister, we're losing the convoy.

SISTER LAFFIN   Florence, we have to go.

FLO   I'm coming. *(To LT DAVIES)* I can't, not now,
                     I'm on my way to Doullens. Write to me.
                     I have to go.

LT DAVIES   No wait. I remember something.

*LT DAVIES stops her, kisses her again — more hoots and cheers
from the troops.*

CANADIAN OFFICER   We have to keep moving!

Sound of the lorry starting up again. SISTER LAFFIN gets back on lorry.

SISTER LAFFIN   She won't be a moment.

                     (To FLO) Flo, you have to come now.

FLO   Please?! I just need a minute.

CANADIAN OFFICER   Catch us up. Lorry hop. We can't wait.

Lorry drives off.

SISTER LAFFIN   (*Calling back*) Run, you'll probably beat us there. All this mud!

LT DAVIES   Marry me. Marry me — I haven't seen you in nearly a year — marry me here and now, there's a church down the road and we can have a few hours as man and wife. They've gone off without you.

Someone calls out — "Put him out of his misery love".

A few hours alone before I go back.

Troops call out "Say yes" — "Go on, love" — "Run".

FLO   I can't. Not now. If I marry you, they'll send me home. I don't want to — William, we hardly know each other.

LT DAVIES   I knew the moment I saw you.

FLO   Right now there is nothing I would like more than to be your wife. But I can't. I need to finish — I can't leave.

Troops call out — "Breaking his heart love".

Come to me on your next leave? I have to go. Write to me.

She kisses him and runs away.

(*Calling out*) Be good.

LT DAVIES   (*Calling out*) Be safe.

He walks back to a chorus of commiserations — "Plenty of fish in the sea" — "There'll be others mate" — "Heartbreaker".

ACT FIVE | SCENE 3

Convalescent ward, No. 3 Canadian Stationary Hospital,
Citadel of DOULLENS, FRANCE.

8pm, 24 December 1917.

FLO   (*Bandaging SERGEANT JENKINS' eyes*)
                                      24th of December, 1917, Doullens. There is no
                                      controlling chaos. Who comes into your life,
                                      who goes out. When you least expect it. Harry
                                      Jenkins stumbled into the gas ward. Skin on
                                      fire, eyes yellowed and oozing. No oranges,
                                      no songs, barely audible. Not a memory.
                                      Flesh. Promoted to Sergeant.

                                      We met over three Christmases ago.

FLO leads SERGEANT JENKINS to a chair.

JENKINS   Tell me more about Mary? She only wrote me
                                      a few times.

FLO   She got sick on Lemnos last Christmas and
                                      had to go home. She wrote a while ago saying
                                      she was trying to get back here, but I haven't
                                      had a letter for a while now.

                                      I'll let you know if I hear anything. She was a
                                      little soft on you.

Jenkins   More than a little soft.

SISTER LAFFIN carrying Christmas garland is led in by Canadians
MAJOR WALLACE LEONARD and MATRON KATHERINE HALL who
are carrying a gramophone and an unopened bottle of champagne and
two glasses. He is wearing a Christmas hat and they are singing "Deck
Miss Hall with Boughs of Holly".

Both the MAJOR and MATRON are clearly a little intoxicated.

MAJOR LEONARD	Merry Christmas to all of you!
FLO	Merry Christmas, Major Leonard, Miss Hall. Giggle.
MATRON HALL	And to you, dear! To you all!
SISTER LAFFIN	A little too merry.
JENKINS	Thank you.
MAJOR LEONARD	(*Cranking the gramophone, the song is 'Fidgety Feet'*) Who's for a dance? Miss Hall — Katherine — may I have the honour?
MATRON HALL	Why certainly, Wallace. (*To Flo about Jenkins*) Sergeant Jenkins, join us — help him Sister Whiting.
FLO	Let's dance, Harry. I'll lead, if I can.

They dance. SISTER LAFFIN dances on her own quite happily.

MATRON HALL	(*To SISTER LAFFIN*) Go and get someone to dance with, Eunice.
SISTER LAFFIN	I'm fine, thank you.
MATRON HALL	How could I forget — we found champagne in the cellar! Open another, Wallace, open it! (*To SISTER LAFFIN*) Get more glasses, we'll all have a drink!

SISTER LAFFIN takes up the glasses as MAJOR LEONARD opens the champagne. The cork pops loudly. They cheer in delight and SISTER LAFFIN tries to catch the spilling champagne.

JENKINS tears at his bandages and violently throws FLO to the floor. He pins her down, sitting on her chest and punches her once in the face.

MAJOR LEONARD, MATRON HALL and SISTER LAFFIN try to assist but JENKINS takes a grenade from his pocket and pulls the pin.

He throws the pin away and threatens them all with the live grenade.

FLO reaches for the grenade but JENKINS punches her unconscious with his free hand. JENKINS screams at the unconscious FLO, threatening her and all who come near him.

SISTER LAFFIN   *(Screaming)* No! Harry, it's Flo. Stop.

JENKINS slows then stops. He puts his face close to FLO's. He gets off her and tries to pick her up. He can't.

MAJOR LEONARD   *(To MATRON HALL)* Get her out of here.

FLO becomes conscious as MATRON HALL and SISTER LAFFIN struggle to get her out.

Calm down, son. Calm down. Everything will be all right. We'll find the pin. *(MAJOR LEONARD moves in the direction JENKINS threw the pin)* Everything will be fine.

JENKINS   *(Backing away, to himself)* I'm sorry, Flo.

He releases the lever on the grenade and holds it close to himself. About four seconds later, it explodes. All is dark.

ACT FIVE | SCENE 4

A ward for sick nursing sisters, DOULLENS.

Late at night, 9 January 1918.

SISTER LAFFIN helps FLO into her bed. FLO sits surrounded by letters that she was writing but has been unable to finish, letters she has received, parcels, photos and trinkets. CAPTAIN DAVIES moves out of the shadows.

CAPTAIN DAVIES   My love, I have been promoted to Captain. A sudden vacancy opened up. I haven't heard from you in a fortnight. What news? I am pushing for leave in February if all goes well. Can I come to you? I will ask you to marry me again. It is a tradition I like to keep up and you will find a ring with this letter. *(She takes out the ring, puts it on her finger)* It is a shabby and pathetic thing, but will you accept it as a promise? Not for now, but for the future. It can mean everything or nothing to you. To me it means the world.

CAPTAIN DAVIES exits. FLO writes home.

FLO   January 9th, 1918, Doullens. Dear father, I am engaged, I think.

A toddler is heard laughing. MR WHITING is reading and calling out to his wife.

MR WHITING   She's engaged!

He holds an open package and reads a letter — there is a small toy nurse in the package.

FLO   His name is William Davies and he has just been promoted to Captain. I am so proud of him. We have been writing for years,

I met him in Cairo.

MR WHITING   She met him in Cairo!

FLO   He will want to ask your permission.

MR WHITING   He wants to ask my permission!

FLO   Please say yes.

MR WHITING   Should I say yes?

FLO   The toy is for little Flossie.

I was to rejoin the 3rd but I have been
accepted into a new course. Eight weeks
studying anaesthetics at the First British
General Hospital, Étretat. One of only
23 Australians to be chosen. Miss Watson
has seen to it, and says Mary will be
joining us both and we will soon be a
team once more. It will be so good to
see them all again. Much love, Flo.

FLO writes a letter to Mrs Jenkins.

FLO   Dear Mrs Jenkins, The *Kyarra* has come
to mean a lot of things to me. But mostly I
remember it is where I met so many fine boys,
including Harry — in his element — while
I was out of mine. I knew him for such a
short time but we become a close group
and I will be forever proud and grateful to
call him friend. I will always think of him
singing, putting cherries on his ears, ready
for a laugh. Thank you for raising such a
wonderful grandson. Florence Whiting.

*FLO puts the ring on a string around her neck and
hides it under her clothes. She places the beaded necklace
in with the letter to Mrs. Jenkins.*

ACT FIVE | SCENE 5

Surgical tent, 2nd Australian Casualty Clearing Station, BLENDECQUES, near Saint-Omer, FRANCE.

8.10pm, 25 July 1918.

Heavy shelling can be heard a few miles off. The night sky is illuminated by flashes and flares.

MATRON WATSON, wearing a helmet and carrying a lantern, ushers FLO and COLONEL TERREY, also wearing helmets, into the sandbagged surgical tent with electric lights. A patient, SERGEANT LITTLE ('SHORTY') lies conscious on the operating table.

SHORTY	Hurry up, would you! Feel safer in a trench.
MATRON WATSON	*(To Shorty)* The shells are miles away. *(To FLO)* You three are late. Wait, where is Sister Douglas? *(SISTER DOUGLAS rushes in)* Where's your helmet?
SISTER DOUGLAS	I went back for it, Miss Watson, but the shells seemed so close this time. I turned around but you were all gone. But I'm here now.
MATRON WATSON	*(Handing helmet to SISTER DOUGLAS)* Wear mine. *(Addressing the room)* As usual, we're working in tandem with the First Australian across the field. We are open until we are full, then they take over.
COL TERREY	Understood, we're used to all this by now. Let's get this traveling circus underway, Sisters. Have a good night, Miss Watson.

MATRON WATSON   Goodnight, Colonel Terrey. Sisters. *(Exiting)*
                     Don't be late again.

COL TERREY   My fault, Miss Watson. It won't happen again.

FLO   *(To SHORTY)* How much do you weigh?

SHORTY   10 stone 3, Sister, and I'm 5 foot 5.

FLO   You've done this before.

SHORTY   Once or twice. I used to be six foot.

COL TERREY   Under you go then.

FLO   Take a few deep breaths for me.

SHORTY goes under.

FLO   He's under, Colonel.

COL TERREY   Humerus is unbroken, but there is extensive
                     tissue damage.

He extracts a tooth.

                     Does he have all his teeth, Sister Whiting?

FLO examines his mouth, he has no missing teeth.

FLO   Yes, all there.

COL TERREY   *(Discarding the tooth into a dish)* Clean that
                     up for me.

SISTER DOUGLAS sponges up the blood.

SISTER DOUGLAS   I don't think any of this is his either, Colonel.

COL TERREY   Yes, he appears to be wearing someone else.

	Must see if we can get over to say hello to the First. Should have done it weeks ago. Will be good to see old Murphy and Fenton again.
	Lay the drainage tube a little lower.
	Do you have friends at the First, Sister Whiting?
FLO	Should do.
COL TERREY	You, Sister Douglas?
SISTER DOUGLAS	Yes, Olive Moffat is there, or at least she was a week ago. Shall we walk over tomorrow afternoon before we go on shift again?
FLO	Let's do that.
COL TERREY	I'll escort you. Let's meet in front of the Officers' Mess about five. We can walk across together.

COLONEL TERREY begins to dress the wound when a loud shell bursts and all the lights go out.

| | Dammit! We're almost finished. I'll find out — |

He is met by MATRON WATSON at the door, she carries a note. All is dark.

	Miss Watson?
MATRON WATSON	I have a message —
COL TERREY	I'll take it.

The lights flicker back on.

MATRON WATSON	No.

MATRON WATSON walks towards FLO, who backs away.

*MATRON WATSON hands an envelope to FLO who cannot bring herself
to read the message. She hands the message back to MATRON WATSON,
silently giving her permission to read it.*

MATRON WATSON   Captain William Davies. Died of wounds
                       17th July, 1918. Buried near Villers-
                       Bretonneux.

MATRON WATSON turns and talks to COLONEL TERREY.

                       Is there much to do?

COL TERREY   Just the dressing.

MATRON WATSON   Finish.

*COLONEL TERREY and SISTER DOUGLAS finish dressing the patient's
wound. MATRON WATSON moves away from FLO.*

                       I will get Barker and Wicks to assist you,
                       Colonel.

*COLONEL TERREY exits. SISTER DOUGLAS silently monitors the
patient. MATRON WATSON stands head bowed.*

*FLO moves away and takes off her helmet. A bright morning light
brings her into focus. She has walked until dawn. She stands alone in a
field — Nouveau-Monde, near Armentieres, France.*

*FLO catches her breath and removes her veil. Reaching into her apron
pocket, she takes out the Princess Mary tin. Opening it, we see the tin
stuffed with her letters from LT DAVIES and the dried poppy fragments.
She places the death message into the tin along with the engagement ring.*

Closing the lid, she stands for a moment before putting her veil back on.

ACT FIVE | SCENE 6

2nd Australian Casualty Clearing Station, in an open field, NOUVEAU-MONDE near ARMENTIERES, FRANCE.

11am, 11 November 1918.

A tented ward full of influenza patients. Bells begin to peal, cheering can be heard outside. SISTER DOUGLAS is treating an AMERICAN SOLDIER who is struggling to breathe.

SISTER DOUGLAS — Try not to breathe too fast, America, just gently, gently. That's it — good — try to stay calm. Small gentle breaths.

FLO and MATRON WATSON enter.

Have you heard anything? Is it done? Sounds like a wedding out there. Surely it's over?

FLO — I think so. It's just passed eleven o'clock.

SISTER DOUGLAS — Not sure I want to go home.

FLO — No, I'm ready.

MATRON WATSON — Best we just keep working.

MATRON WATSON AND FLO move to seat the endless stream of patients. SISTER DOUGLAS continues to attend to the AMERICAN SOLDIER.

Bagpipes playing 'Flowers of the Forest' can be heard.

THE END

Captain R. P. Henley and Sisters, No. 3 Australian CCS, Brandhoek.

May Tilton, 'The Grey Battalion.'

Matron Grace Wilson.
No. 3 Australian General Hospital, Abbassia, 1916.
Photo: A.W. Savage. Mitchell Library, State Library of New South Wales, PXE 698.

GLOSSARY

AANS, Australian Army Nursing Service

Army reserve unit, part of the Australian Army Medical Corps, for trained female nurses. A candidate for enrolment as Sister had to be between 21 and 40 years of age, single or a widow, with not less than three years' training in medical and surgical nursing in a recognised civil hospital, or holding a certificate in general nursing or accreditation from a nursing association.

AGH, Australian General Hospital

Base hospital with over 1,000 beds. The 1st AGH served in Cairo (Heliopolis), then on the Western Front at Rouen, France. The 2nd also served in Cairo, at Mena House, then in France at Wimereux. The 3rd AGH was landed on the island of Lemnos in August 1915 during the Gallipoli Campaign. From April 1917, it was based in France at Abbeville.

Blendecques

Town in northern France. The 2nd Australian Casualty Clearing Station was located here between 14 April and 31 August 1918, alongside No. 1 Australian CCS. In June and July 1918, these two hospitals admitted some 8,000 casualties, sick and wounded.

Capeline bandage

Covers the head or an amputation stump like a cap.

CCS, Casualty Clearing Station

Field hospital to triage and stabilise wounded soldiers before they can be transported to rear hospitals for further treatment. Nominally 200 beds. The 2nd Australian CCS reached France with the Australian Imperial Force in 1916. The official history states that they were established almost literally 'in the front line.'

Christmas billy

Hampers produced in Australia by the Australian Comforts Fund and the Red Cross for soldiers overseas. The 'comforts', which included things like tobacco, knitted socks, writing paper, tinned fruit and cake, were packed in a billy.

Doullens

French town behind the Somme battlefields of the First World War. No. 3 Canadian Stationary Hospital was located in the grounds of its large 16th century Citadel. An Australian nursing sister, Elsie Tranter, was detached to this hospital from March to May 1918. Three sisters were killed and one seriously wounded in an air raid at the end of May 1918.

Gascon

Hospital ship. Was off Anzac Cove receiving casualties from the Gallipoli Landing on 25 April 1915. Seven Australian nurses and a British matron were on-board. The ex-passenger steamer had been fitted up for 350 patients, and mattresses were laid down to accommodate 150 more. When *Gascon* reached Alexandria on 28 April, 535 wounded were unloaded. Soldiers who had died aboard ship were buried at sea.

Kyarra

Hospital ship. Embarked for Egypt in November 1914 with the staff and equipment of the 1st and 2nd AGH, 1st and 2nd Australian Stationary Hospitals, and No. 1 Australian Casualty Clearing Station. Converted into a troop transport in March 1915. Sunk by a German submarine off the English coast in May 1918.

Lemnos

An island in the Aegean Sea, some 120 kilometres sailing distance from Anzac Cove. Because of its great, natural harbour, the town of Mudros (and its environs) became the principal base of the Mediterranean Expeditionary Force during the Gallipoli Campaign. The 3rd Australian General Hospital was located at West Mudros, on a narrow peninsula known as Turks Head.

Matron

The most senior nurse in a hospital.

Nouveau-Monde

Between Estaires and Laventie, in northern France.
No. 2 Australian CCS was located in a field at Nouveau-Monde
during October–November 1918, as the medical services pushed
forward with the advancing Allied armies.

Onbaşı

Rank of corporal in the Ottoman Army. Pronounced on-bash-uh.

Orderly

Typically a man in the Australian Army Medical Corps. Some had
St John Ambulance first aid training or nursing experience. General
duty orderlies helped with tasks such as heavy lifting, carrying patients
and stores. Others were assigned as nursing or medical orderlies,
working closely with the female nurses.

Princess Mary tin

A brass tin with small gifts, given at Christmas to soldiers, sailors
and nurses. The tin was decorated with an image of King George V's
17-year-old daughter, Mary.

Sister

Trained nurse. First level of promotion within the AANS.

SN, Staff Nurse

Trained nurse. Entry-level status in the AANS. Less seniority than
a Sister, although known by that title.

Wimereux

French coastal town on the English channel about 5 kilometres north
of Boulogne, one of the most important First World War base ports.
No. 2 AGH was located at Wimereux from July 1916 to February 1919.
The area was heavily bombed by German aircraft.

No. 3 Australian General Hospital, Lemnos.
Sister Evelyn Davies in wet-weather gear with lantern.
Australian War Memorial, A05374.

RECOMMENDED READING

Personal accounts

In all those lines : the diary of Sister Elsie Tranter 1916–1919, edited by J. M. Gillings & J. Richards (2008)

Kitty's war : the remarkable wartime experiences of Kit McNaughton, Janet Butler (University of Queensland Press, 2013)

Letters of an Australian army sister, Anne Donnell (Angus & Robertson, 1920)

Matron Ida Greaves : 'a right daughter of Australia', Christine M. Bramble, 2021

The grey battalion, May Tilton (Angus & Robertson, 1933)

The life and letters of Elizabeth McMillan : 1882–1943, edited by Clare Ashton (Anchor Books, 2021)

We are here, too : the diaries and letters of Sister Olive L. C. Haynes, November 1914 to February 1918, edited by Margaret O. Young (2014)

Nurses' narratives, Records of A. G. Butler, Historian of Australian Army Medical Services, Australian War Memorial, AWM41

Histories

Guns and brooches : Australian Army nursing from the Boer War to the Gulf War, Jan Bassett (Oxford University Press, 1992)

More than bombs and bandages : Australian Army nurses at work in World War I, Kirsty Harris (Big Sky Publishing, 2011)

Nightingales in the mud : the Digger sisters of the Great War, 1914–1918, Marianne Barker (Allen & Unwin, 1989)

The other Anzacs : nurses at war, 1914–18, Peter Rees (Allen & Unwin, 2008)

Veiled lives : threading Australian nursing history into the fabric of the First World War, Ruth Rae (The College of Nursing, 2009)

www.ingramcontent.com/pod-product-compliance
Lightning Source LLC
Chambersburg PA
CBHW070341120726
47909CB00008B/2709